JIMMY the JITTERY JITTERBUG

by

Sonica Ellis

Illustrated by Harriet Rodis

Jimmy is a Jitterbug, the sweetest, kindest and the most loving little Jitterbug you would ever want to meet.

But Jimmy is often shy and anxious, and when Jimmy is anxious, he jitters.

Jimmy jitters at school when it's his turn to read. He is worried that his classmates will laugh at him if he gets a word wrong, or that he might read too quickly or too slowly, or too softly, or too loudly.

"Jimmy, everything is fine," said his teacher, Miss Hoot, reassuring him. "There is no need to rush and nothing to worry about. We are all enjoying very much listening to you read."

That made Jimmy feel better and he finished his reading without quite so much jittering.

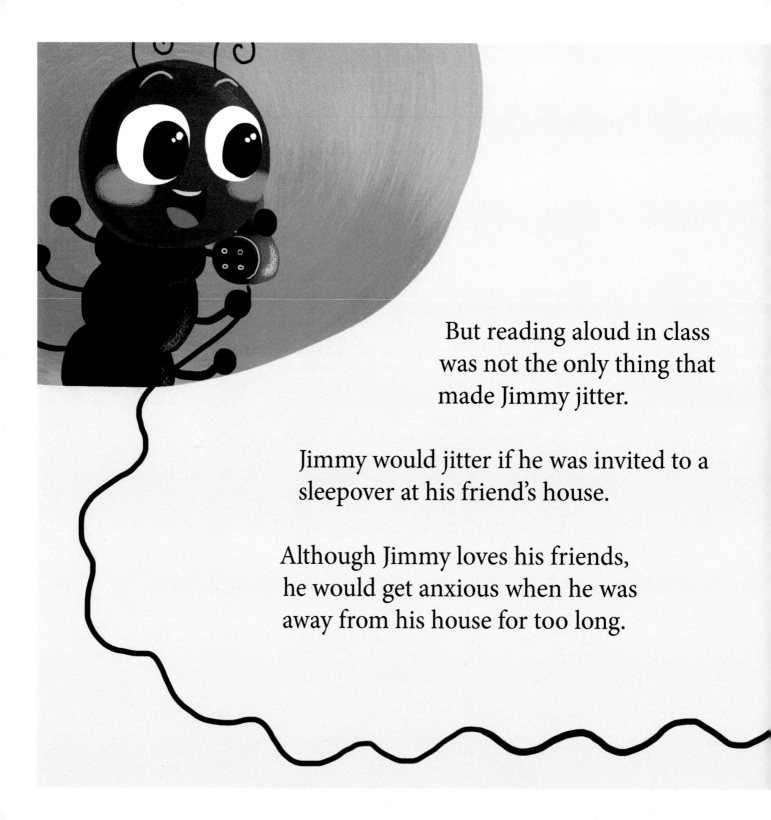

But reading aloud in class was not the only thing that made Jimmy jitter.

Jimmy would jitter if he was invited to a sleepover at his friend's house.

Although Jimmy loves his friends, he would get anxious when he was away from his house for too long.

"Momma, maybe I should'nt go.
Who will water the plants or take
out the trash when I am gone?

What if I am not having fun?

What…What if I get hurt?

Who would take care of you if I'm
gone? "

asked Jimmy as he jittered

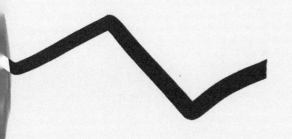

"Now Jimmy," replied his mother softly "I can certainly take care of the plants and trash, and both you and I are going to be absolutely fine.

You love your friends and they love you. I am certain that in no time at all you will be having more fun than you will know what to do with!"

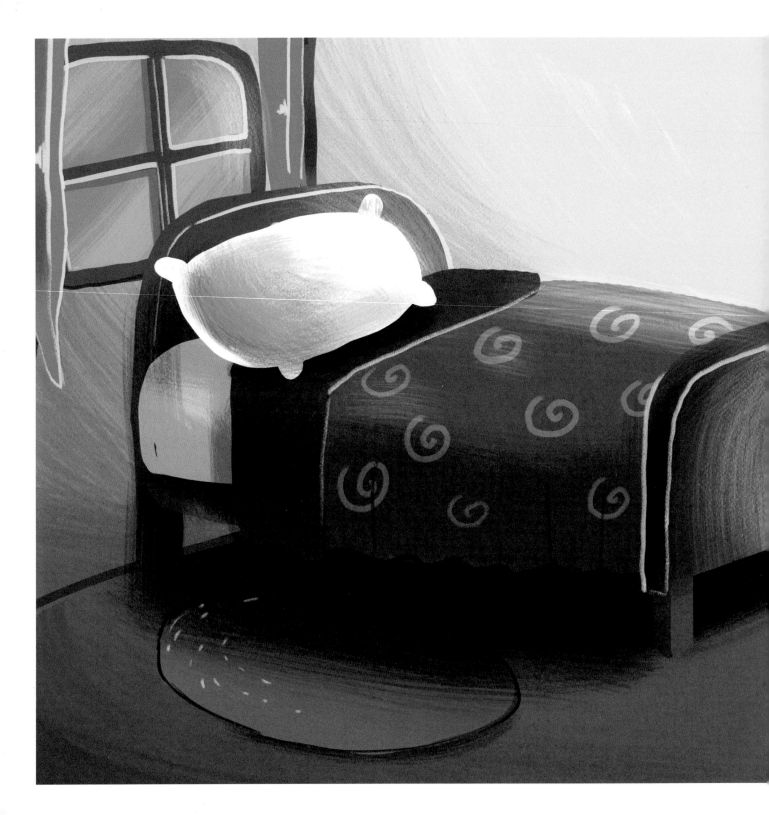

That made Jimmy relax and he happily packed up his things for the sleepover without quite so much jittering.

But that wasn't all of Jimmy's worries.

Jimmy would also jitter at bedtime.

"It is so dark. I cannot see anything.

What if there are monsters that are going to get me?"

said Jimmy as he jittered.

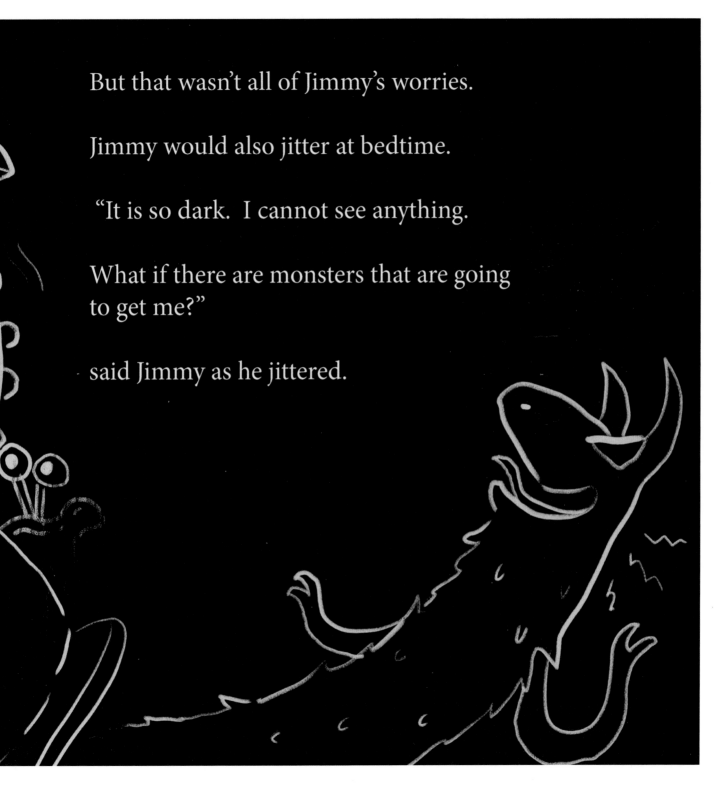

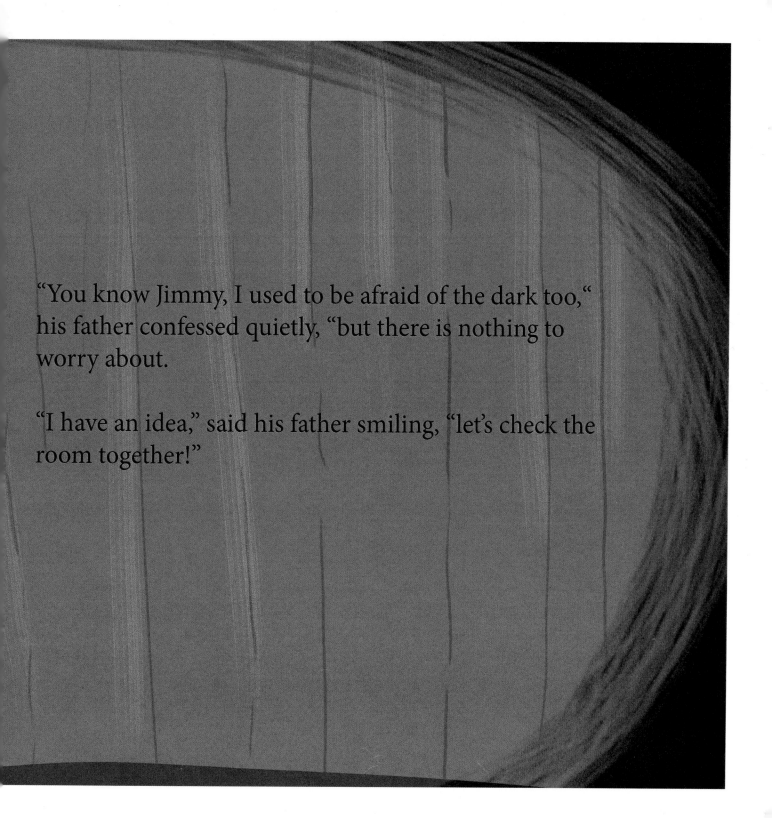

"You know Jimmy, I used to be afraid of the dark too," his father confessed quietly, "but there is nothing to worry about.

"I have an idea," said his father smiling, "let's check the room together!"

And with that Jimmy and his father checked the closets,
behind the curtains, and under the bed
and not a single monster was to be found.

"Did you find anything Jimmy?" asked his father, already knowing the answer.

"No Papa" said Jimmy as he climbed into his bed.

"Well then, the coast is clear" said Jimmy's father giving him a little tickle as he tucked him in.

"And do not worry, I will put this little night light here next to your bed so it is not quite so dark." And with that he gave Jimmy a goodnight kiss.

That made Jimmy feel better, and he did not jitter quite so much.

Intentional Read-Aloud

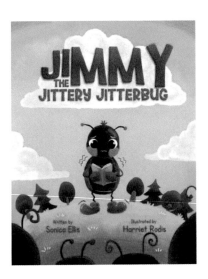

Before Reading

- Take a look at the cover. What do you think this story will be about? What do you think the character will do?

Discussion Questions

- Who is the main character?

- How would you describe him?

- What other characters are in the book?

- What things make Jimmy jitter?

- In the story, Jimmy's parents and teacher help him find ways to calm his jitters. What are some other strategies Jimmy could try when he jitters in the future?

Name: _____

Directions: In "Jimmy the Jittery Jitterbug", there are three things that made him jittery. Which event happened first, second and third in the story?

Word Bank		
Bedtime	Sleepovers	Reading out loud

First: _____

Second: _____

Third:_____

Knowing the three events that made Jimmy jitter, predict what other events might make him jitter in the future. Provide a solution to your prediction!

_____

_____

_____

Name: _____

When Jimmy Jitterbug is anxious, he jitters.
What events or situations make you jitter?

_____

_____

_____

_____

_____

_____

_____

_____

_____

_____

_____

Made in the USA
San Bernardino, CA
27 April 2020